Sa

Dragon Skulls MC

The Dark Side

by
Kyra Nyx
and
Euryia Larsen

Description

Chastity Morgan

I haven't seen my sperm donor since I was in kindergarten. Yet now the Dragon Skulls MC expects me to repay his debt. Like hell, I will. I'm no shrinking violet or damsel in distress. Saint is going to learn real fast that I will not be held accountable for my father's sins.

Luciano "Saint" Telos

The smile of a saint, the soul of a devil. That infamous smile hides the darkness inside. That darkness runs the Dragon Skulls MC, keeping my brothers safe with money in their pockets. No one will ever be allowed to betray us, to steal from us. Those that do are dealt with harshly.

Chapter 1

Saint

I cocked my gun, looking the man in the eye, knowing I could kill him with a simple pull of my finger. I could see his fear, smell it, even taste it feeding the darkness inside me. This shit for brains thought he could double-cross my club and me. Stealing from me will get you dead. Killing one of the club girls to use her as a scapegoat was cowardly, and that will get you time with Razor before you die. At least, it usually would.

Tonight, the darkness craved his blood and his fear. It demanded vengeance for taking what belonged to me. It'd been too long since I'd fed it. I sneered at the traitor and ordered, "Take him to the basement. Razor, prepare him *only*."

"Fuck," Razor growled. He was a man of few words, and while I knew he was loyal to me, I never allowed anyone to openly complain or question my decisions.

I narrowed my eyes at him. He recognized the craving, the growing darkness, because he lived for it. Raising a hand in surrender, he bent his head.

I smirked at him. "Don't worry Razor, you'll get your piece." Looking around the club, I ordered, "Ranks to the basement in five." No one betrayed the club and lived. This would provide a fine example of the consequences.

I went to the bar and without needing to say a word,a glass of top-shelf whiskey was handed to me. Savoring the first sip, my mind slipped to Kitty. She was my favorite club girl, and she was loyal. Club girls are protected, and Burn would pay for what he did.

Downing the rest, I slammed the glass down on the bartop and headed to the basement. Time to take care of business. The stairs were narrow, and lowered into a typical dark and damp space.

This basement was anything but ordinary. A large concrete room with several drains, I could smell the bleach used to deep clean the space. My eyes and nose burned from it and I hated it. Unfortunately, it was a necessary evil in this life.

I stepped into the room and looked over at Burn, filled with disgust. He was squealing like a stuck pig, and we'd yet to begin. He was hanging by his wrists, using a secure chain, over one of the floor studs. These weren't like the chains in my playroom. There weren't any cuffs meant to protect the delicate skin of a woman's wrist. Razor could care less if the chains wrapped around his victims hurt.

I stood with my arms crossed, and waited patiently for all ranked members to appear. They walked around Burn as they came down the stairs and formed a circle surrounding him. Excommunication from the club as well as execution of any punishments had to be witnessed by all Ranks.

I looked around the room as my VP, Scar, finally joined us. "Ready to have some fun?" I asked him in a low voice. His simple grunt didn't surprise me and made me chuckle. Scar hated this shit, always had.

Becoming serious, I stood in front of Burn as I looked at each and every club officer. "As we voted upon, Burn has been found guilty of theft of club funds, theft of club property, and the murder of Kitty, one of the club girls."

As one, all the officers declared, "Aye!"

"Punishment is the removal of all colors and permanent removal from the club."

"Aye!"

I've been told I have the smile of a saint and the soul of a devil. That same smile appeared on my face now, edged with danger as I turned to look at Burn. As soon as he saw it, he started to panic, flailing back and forth, begging for his life.

"Pres, please, you have to believe me. I didn't do any of that. You know me. I'm as loyal as they come."

Ignoring his pleas, I pulled out my knife, using it to slice through the leather and remove his cut.. I dropped it into a nearby metal barrel for burning when we were finished. I took a step back as Razor and Rake, our Treasurer, stripped him down until he was naked, everything placed into the same barrel.

As he hung there, I simply stood watching him. The tears came next. Sometimes, they pissed themselves before the tears, but I should have known that Burn was a crying pussy. He was still begging and pleading but I didn't acknowledge him. The darkness had taken over.

I grabbed Burn's tiny cock in my hand and removed it from his body with a simple flick of my knife. Razor stepped forward and forced Burns mouth open, and I shoved his cock inside, forcing it down into his throat, making it harder to spit it out and cutting off his cries.

Reaching down again, I removed each of his balls. Lifting them up to show him, I tossed them to Razor's bulldog, Chewy, who ate them as if they were the finest canine delicacy.

Glancing down, I watched as blood poured from where his cock and balls used to be, puddling beneath him as it trickled down the drain. Looking up at his face, I smirked at the sack of shit.

Looking at my men, I instructed, "Remove his colors piece by piece. Leave his back to Razor." I stepped out of the way and leaned against a table near the barrel. Pulling out my pack of cigarettes, I lit one up while I watched the action. I was working on quitting, being down to one a day. The exception was days like today.

Each time the motherfucker screamed in pain, each time he begged for mercy, I felt the darkness grow a little bit stronger. These were musical sounds to the ears of the monster inside me. This would be a reminder to all, of the consequences of fucking the club over, and crossing me. I may look like a nice guy, but nothing could be further from the truth.

I noticed Razor walking over to the table that held his favorite toys. I watched intrigued as he picked up a kitchen blow torch and checked fuel levels as well as making sure it would stay lit. He felt my eyes on him and turned to look at me, smirking. "His name will fit now."

I chuckled as he approached the last club tattoo on Burn's body. It dawned on me what he was doing and where I'd seen it before. "I thought you hated that show?"

Razor shrugged. "What can I say, Sons of Anarchy had some good ideas." I watched as the colored skin bubbled and popped from the heat of the torch to the sound of Burn's screams. Every time he passed out, Razor would pause while the guys threw ice water in his face, then Razor would begin again.

The smell of burnt flesh was even worse than bleach. It was disgusting. For a motherfucker like Burn, who had more alcohol in him than anything else, it smelled even worse. Finally, Razor turned off the torch and stepped back as he nodded to me.

Standing up I approached the man that was barely hanging on to life. Grabbing hold of his face, I carved a dragon into his cheek before whispering in his ear, "I'll make sure I say hello to that daughter of yours." What little fight remaining in him rose up, but it was of no use. Taking my pistol from its holder under my cut, I looked straight into Burn's terror filled eyes and shot him in the forehead.

"Razor, take care of this. Use Slay if you need help to dispose of him. Use the prospects to clean the basement. Scar, you and Rake bring me the girl. I want my money and product and I'm betting she knows where it's at." They all nodded before I went upstairs to get a drink and take a shower. I could smell his stench on me.

Chapter 2

Chastity

Looking at the time, I groaned as I pulled into 7 Deadly Sins, the tattoo parlor where I worked. I was late. Anytime I had to be there before eleven a.m. I ended up late. I hated mornings with a passion, always had. My mom used to say that my opinion of mornings was the only thing that I got from my dad. I was a night owl through and through, just like him.

I yawned as I opened the back door and before it had even closed, Ella Lynn, my boss and best friend, was handing me a coffee. "Bless you, oh great and wondrous boss."

Ella snorted at me. "I don't know why you schedule these early appointment times for yourself. They always make you so miserable." "I'm probably a masochist. Why are you here so early?"

"I figured I'd keep you company while I catch up on paperwork. Speaking of, you got another piece of fan mail."

I looked at the handwritten name and address on the envelope as I took it from her outstretched hand. "I really hope it's not another letter from the guys at the state prison. Those are way too creepy." She laughed at me, settling into my visitor chair, wanting to see who it was from.

I examined the envelope taking note of the lack of return address and breathed a sigh of relief when I didn't see the state prison mail stamp. Opening it up, I pulled out a handwritten letter, a key falling free. I picked it up and examined it. It was a normal nondescript key.

Looking at the letter, I quickly skimmed over it until my eyes fell on the one name I never expected or wanted to see."Fuck,"

"Who's it from?" Ella asked, trying to read it upside down.

"My father," I whispered, as I sank down onto my stool to read the letter.

My dearest Chastity,

I know that I'm a horrible father but I beg you to read this letter. If you received it then I'm probably dead. I fucked up, baby girl. I fucked up real bad.

I crossed the club and made it worse by killing Saint's piece. You need to run, and run now. I put everything you'll need in a locker at the address below. Take it and disappear otherwise he'll come for you and kill you as well.

Saint is a monster and will wipe out my family, which is only you. So I beg of you to do as I ask. I always loved you.

I'm sorry,
Burn - Chris Beard

My hand was shaking when I finished the letter. The last time I'd heard from my sperm donor was when I was five and he took me to school. I never saw him again after that. Heck, I figured he was probably dead or in jail. The chime signaling the front door went off, scaring the shit out of me.

Shoving the key into my pocket, I turned to see two large men walking toward Ella and me. One was older with a nasty looking scar on his cheek. His shaggy salt and pepper hair, hard eyes, and motorcycle cut made me wonder if these were the guys Burn warned me about. The other guy was hot as sin. His long black hair and scowl were just Ella's type, which was why I was unsurprised at her sharp intake of breath beside me.

I couldn't run so I decided to play it cool. "Morning, wanting to get a tattoo or piercing?"

"Neither. I'm Scar, this is Rake. Chastity Morgan, can we talk in private?"

"Ella's cool. We're up in each other's business daily. How can I help you, gentlemen?"

Rake looked over at Scar who nodded subtly to the younger man. My eyes narrowed. I didn't trust these men at all.

"Your dad, Burn…"

"Burn?" I interrupted, playing dumb. "My sperm donor is Chris Beard. He wasn't any father to me. I haven't seen the cocksucker since he left after dropping me off for the first day of kindergarten."

"Chris, or Burn as we knew him, is dead."

I stood there blinking at them, showing no emotion. It wasn't acting, I truly felt nothing for the man. "Okay, thanks for letting me know but a phone call would have worked too. As you can tell, I could give a rat's ass if he is dead, alive, or in jail being used as a fuck toy."

Their expressions darkened at my words and I knew I wasn't going to like what was said next. "We're going to need both you ladies to come with us."

"Oh hell no! I have a business to run, Mr. Scar. Tell your boss, or whoever sent you, to come to see us," Ella said. At five foot nothing she looked like a little girl about to stomp her feet and throw a tantrum with her long brown hair in a ponytail and her golden eyes flashing with her anger.

"Ma'am, neither Scar nor I want to hurt you ladies but you *will* come with us, now," Scar growled, looking directly at Ella.

"Rake, take Ms. Boss Lady to close up the shop. Chastity and I need to chat."

I watched as Rake took Ella by the arm toward the front of the shop to lock up. Looking back at Scar, I folded my arms across my chest and asked, "Why the hell are you kidnapping us? I haven't seen this Burn since I was in kindergarten like I told you. I have nothing to do with him or his life."

"We know he left everything to you. He stole from the club and Saint wants what he's owed, one way or another. Take a piece of advice, Chastity. Saint is *not* someone you want to mess with."

"Fine," I huffed. Grabbing my purse, I dropped the letter and key inside. I had a feeling I was going to need them. Turning around, I got right into Scar's personal space. "I don't fucking care who this asshole boss is, but I'm not Burn and I sure as hell have nothing to do with anything related to him. Don't expect me to do as you say simply because you're a big strong man," venom dripped from every word.

I waited for a response, refusing to blink or back down. Suddenly Scar started chuckling. "Yo Rake, Ms. Morgan here is gonna be fun. Just wait till Saint gets a load of her."

I rode on the back of Scar's motorcycle and Rake had Ella behind him. I could already sense something starting to brew between Rake and Ella, but lord only knew what exactly. Ella attracted men like bees to honey but what she truly wanted was much harder to determine.

Scar was an interesting character. He came off as cold and hard, but when I was looking into his eyes I could tell he was a deep well of hidden emotion. It was obvious life hadn't been easy for him. Try as I might, so far I couldn't hate him. He and Rake were both being respectful, even if they were kidnapping us.

We paused at a red light and Scar asked,, "You alright?"

"Fine. Anything I should know before I meet your big bad boss?" I had to yell so that I could be heard over the motorcycle.

"Don't try to play him. Honesty. You play him, you'll die and so will Ella. Give him what he wants and you might just survive." If this big scary biker thought Saint might kill us, I knew I should be terrified. Unfortunately, how I should react and how I did in reality wasn't always the same.

We'd been riding for a while, leaving the edges of the Dallas/Ft. Worth metroplex. This part of Texas was beautiful, with wide-open spaces and fresh air. When we turned down a lone driveway off the State Highway, I looked around.

Just where were we going? There was nothing around here from what I could see. Scar tapped one of my hands wrapped around his waist and pointed straight ahead. Looking over his shoulder, I watched as we approached a twenty feet tall perimeter fence with a large gate looming in front of us.

This place appeared to be some sort of compound and that made me more nervous than I was willing to admit to myself. Once we drove through the gate I looked around. There were many buildings on the property. I saw large buildings, smaller buildings that looked like homes, motorcycles, biker men, and of course scantily-clad women.

Ready or not, we'd arrived.

Chapter 3

Saint

I watched as Scar and Rake finally arrived with not one, but two women. With one look, they knew I wanted an explanation before I even said a word. Their orders were to bring me one Chastity Morgan. It didn't include 'and friend'.

I assumed that the woman climbing off of Scar's ride was Chastity. There was no way he'd depend on anyone else to bring her in when the order was given to him directly. I watched, my jaw clenching, as he helped her steady herself once she was standing on solid ground. If I didn't know better, I'd say my ice-cold VP already had a soft spot for her and that wasn't sitting well with me.

Watching her approach, I took note of everything about this woman. She was a tiny thing compared to my six-foot-three frame, but her combat boots, ripped jeans, Megadeth shirt, and colorful tattoo sleeves of artwork spoke of her rebellious side. The side I was interested in.

Her dark blue hair was piled high on her head, a riot of curls that looked sexy as fuck. I wasn't a fan of all those clown-ass colors for hair but I had to admit, the blue emphasized the blue fire of her eyes and it looked hot on her. I chuckled to myself at the look of contempt she threw my way. 'Well, little blue, if you hate me now, just wait till I tell you all about dear ole Dad's demise.'

"Office," I ordered, scowling at Scar, silently demanding an explanation. "Either her friend joined the party or died," he shrugged while Chastity gasped in horror and whipped her head around to look at him. I chuckled darkly. If a simple comment like that horrified her, what fun we were going to have.

Scar and Rake placed the girls down on the chairs in front of my desk as I closed the door. Crossing my arms, I stood there staring at Chastity. I was a fan of making people nervous. How they reacted told me what methods would work best to get what I wanted. They usually started to fidget, some would start to sweat, and almost all refused to look me in the eye.

Chastity and her friend did none of that. Chastity sat there, still as a statue, and returned my stare with a dark look of her own. Her friend started to breathe deeper as her anger began to rise. Impressive.

"Why the fuck have we been kidnapped?" the friend asked.

I turned to look at her slowly, ripping my eyes from Chastity. "Shut the fuck up," I snarled at her.

Chastity stood up, Scar forcing her back down before I raised my finger to stop him. From her chair, she growled at me, "Do not talk to her like that. Whatever the reason for this insanity, don't *ever* talk to Ella like that again. You may be some badass biker god in your little kingdom, but where I grew up men treated women with respect."

I started to chuckle at her. Shock passed over her expression when it turned into a full-bodied laugh. I leaned down so that we were practically nose to nose, the laugh stopping as fast as it started. "You may be a hot piece of ass, but the only woman deserving of what you call 'respect' doesn't exist. Respect is earned." Pulling out my pistol, I held it against her forehead. "Your piece of shit father stole from me and my club. I want it back, *NOW*."

Ignoring the gun pointed at her, she spat out, "That sperm donor was no father to me." Before I could blink, her hand shot out and snapped the safety on as she simultaneously ripped my gun out of my hand and tossed it to Ella. While I was distracted, her other hand held a sharp knife that appeared out of nowhere and was now sitting against my cock. "Shall we sit down and discuss this like adults, or do I get to turn you into a eunuch before your men shoot me?"

Fuck, she was hot. Just who was this blue-haired tigress? I knew right then, she would be mine before the day was done. She already fascinated me more than any other woman had. I chuckled again as I stood up from leaning on the desk, ignoring the sharp blade resting against my jeans. I walked around my desk and sat down, propping my feet up and crossing them at the ankles.

Removing the magazine from my pistol, her eyes never leaving me, Ella tossed my gun to me. I smirked when she put the magazine on my desk and slid it to me. I left it where it was. These two women were definitely more entertaining than I expected. The question now demanding an immediate answer was who were these ladies, and where did civilians learn moves like that?

Chastity turned to look at Scar and I found I didn't like that at all. I wanted her attention on me and only me. "May I have my bag?" Scar handed it to her and I watched as she dug into it.

"I haven't seen the man you knew as Burn since the day he dropped me off at kindergarten and ghosted from my life. I want nothing to do with him and his business with you. He sent me this letter which I received and opened this morning. In it, there was also a key."

She pulled a folded note out of her bag and sat it on my desk before moving her arm behind her slowly to show Scar and Rake that she was reaching into her jean pocket. She set the key on top of the letter and pushed both toward me. "Now you have all the information that I do."

I picked up the key and unfolded the letter to read it. "It sounds like him but until I get what belongs to this club, this is far from settled. Rake, you brought her friend, take care of her."

I paused, changing my mind when I noticed the subtle panic in Rake's eyes. He was as loyal as they came. He wanted Ella. "Actually, belay that order. She intrigues me. Put her in a cell until you verify this letter. I'll decide what to do with both of these ladies based on what you find. Send Nora in here."

Rake nodded as he pulled Ella to her feet and led her out of my office. I handed the letter and key to Scar. He nodded as he left, following Rake. That left me with Chastity.

We sat there looking at each other for several long moments. "Chastity Morgan, tattoo artist and wild child. Daughter of Christopher Beard, former member of the Dragon Skulls, now dead. Daughter of Barbie Morgan, reformed addict, upstanding citizen, now dead from cancer."

"All true."

"Explain your moves or it doesn't matter what they find, I'll put a bullet in your head."

"Mom was terrified of Burn and his lifestyle. She worried someone would come for us. She made sure I could handle myself. Ella too." I watched for any tell that let me know she was lying. I could read people as easily as I could read a book. She wasn't.

"The FBI has tried to bring us down so many times it's actually embarrassing for them. Your moves are too good to just be self-defense and too blatant to be FBI. I don't trust you."

"Do you trust anyone?" Her question wasn't sarcastic, it was honest. Truth was, I didn't.

"Trust gets you dead with a knife in your back." There was a single knock on the door before Nora, one of the club girls entered.

"Rake said you wanted to see me, Saint?"

"Take Chastity and put her in the black room. Then bring me a bottle of top shelf Jack," I instructed. I watched as Chastity's eyes narrowed at me, spitting fire. This was going to be fun.

Chapter 4

Chastity

I knew that wherever Nora was taking me couldn't be good. As soon as we'd left Saint's office she turned from meek and submissive in front of him, to straight-up catty bitch. Her clothing, or lack thereof, screamed club whore and it was obvious she wanted Saint. She could have him. As hot as the man was, as wet as he made me, I didn't want or need him in my life. My only concern was getting Ella and myself out of here.

Until I could do that, I had a question I was dying to ask. "So, Nora, why is he called Saint?"

"Cuz he has the soul of a devil. Now shut up and keep walking. Once the guys are finished using every hole, you'll be worth less than a two-dollar whore. I'll have to make popcorn for the show."

"Isn't that what you are?" As soon as that came out of my mouth I knew this was going to be a shit storm and not my wisest move. I just couldn't resist. What type of woman wished being gang-raped on a woman she'd just met. Sickening!

It didn't come as a surprise when Nora, in her stripper heels and nonexistent skirt and top, turned and screamed as she grabbed my hair and punched me in the face. Why I didn't block or duck I wasn't sure. That was going to be her one and only hit though.

Grabbing hold of her fist when she tried to punch me again, I flipped her around and chicken-winged her arm behind her back. I really didn't want anyone here to be an enemy of mine. Enemies were bad no matter how you looked at them.

I just wanted Ella and I to return to our lives, without the worry of being dead or worse, raped, before morning. Unfortunately, with every slap and punch I delivered to Nora I felt that freedom slip through my fingers. Saint would surely kill me now.

I threw Nora to the ground and with a swift kick from my combat boot-clad foot I knew she wouldn't be getting up for a while. Surprisingly, none of the bikers came running to investigate the sounds of our catfight. I could run and try to escape but I doubted I'd find Ella before I was caught. Then there was the fact that we were in a secure compound. I was ignoring the desire to see Saint again. That was just a bad idea any way you looked at it.

Sighing, I sat on the ground and waited for someone to show up. Realizing Nora's one-hit split my bottom lip, I prodded it with my fingers. The bitch got me good.

I heard the sound of heavy boots coming towards me. "She's not dead, just out. Stupid bitch punched me in the face and gave me a fat lip. Kill me if you want but the ho' got what she deserved."

I waited for a response and when none was forthcoming I looked up at a smirking Saint, standing with his arms crossed over his incredibly wide chest. God, the man was wicked hot. "Slay, take Nora to Doc."

Within moments, I was alone with Saint again, our eyes locked on each other. I stood up, looking into what I thought were cold gray eyes, more like storm clouds, hiding what lay inside from view. He took hold of my wrist breaking eye contact and looked at my knuckles. Only then did I realize some were split. With a narrowing of his eyes, he led me down the hall in the direction that Nora and I were originally going.

"What is the black room?" I asked, not really expecting an answer.

Sure enough, none came, but as it turned out, the black room was exactly that. A room all in black. At first glance, I thought it was an empty room with black curtains covering every inch of wall space. It was my guess that the curtains hid the secrets of this room.

"This room is mine alone. Consider it a playroom of sorts."

Nora had been in this room, that's why she knew it. The thought of that shouldn't have bothered me in the least and yet it did. "Why did you have her bring me here? To rape me into submission? To have your men rape me?"

Saint's eyes darkened as he moved closer to me. "We may do a lot of illegal shit, but any Dragon Skull who forces an unwilling woman isn't part of the club for long."

If that was the truth, it eased some of the worry I had for Ella and myself. He'd never answered the question though. So I repeated it. "Why bring me here?"

His free hand reached up and caressed my cheek, his thumb wiping away the last remnant of blood before his fingers curled around the back of my neck. Fisting my hair, he held me so that I couldn't look away from him. His voice was a harsh whisper, "Because, Chastity Morgan, you are by far, the hottest piece of ass that I've seen in a long time and if I don't have to put a bullet in your head, then you'll be mine."

The kiss he gave me was neither gentle or sweet. It was dirty and filled with molten desire. It took over my senses until all that existed was Saint and the feel of his lips on mine. This was a down and dirty fuck me kiss and with every passing moment, I was becoming lost to this man.

He pulled back, breaking the kiss, letting me know that he was in control. As his tongue ran over the split in my lip that I'd forgotten about, I hissed at the sting. Trying to catch my breath, forget about my melted underwear, and not look into his eyes, I noticed he'd moved me closer to one of the curtain walls.

He reached behind me and I heard the sound of chains. Before I could react, a leather cuff had encircled my right wrist. I blinked at it, stunned as he did the same to my left. "What the actual fuck?"

The wicked glint in his eyes made me shudder. I wasn't sure if it was out of desire or fear. I wasn't into this sort of thing, but that didn't mean I hadn't thought about it.

"Until I get back what is owed to my club, you'll remain here. No one will enter without my knowledge and the door will be guarded at all times. You may have a few slick moves, little blue, but you're in my house now."

I watched as he turned and left me there, chained up in some sort of kinky sex room. Surprisingly it didn't have that smell that always seemed to permeate rooms used for sex. Either he had a fantastic cleaner or it'd been a while since he used it. A guy like Saint, I'd bet it was the first option.

I tested out the chains. I could move around the room, but couldn't free myself. The cuffs seemed to have some sort of lock that I'd never seen before. It wasn't like I had a clue how

I'd find Ella and escape this compound without being discovered even if I could get out of them.

Did I really want to? Of course I did. Just because Saint excites me doesn't make him the right guy for me. Even as I thought about all the ways he was completely wrong for me, a small but persistent voice in my head whispered how right he was. How much I wanted to get to know the man hidden behind the mask with the tight hot ass.

Looking around, I started to explore the room. Behind each curtain was a surprise. The first door I came across was a small bathroom. At least I wouldn't have to hold it until I peed myself, that was a plus. The next door I discovered was actually a king-size murphy bed hidden away. The rest hid sex toys, some I'd never seen before but could imagine what they were meant for. The remaining curtains seemed to hide nothing at all.

Settling down on the floor against a curtain wall, I thought about my current predicament and hoped my best friend was okay. Closing my eyes I allowed myself a moment of fear. All my life my mother had hammered into my head that I needed to think on my feet and protect myself. I couldn't depend on a man to save me. She taught me I had to be the hero in my own story.

Wiping away the errant tear that escaped, I took a deep steadying breath. While there was an obvious coldness to Saint,I didn't believe that if I cooperated with him that he would kill me and Ella. Closing my eyes and thought about the President of the Dragon Skulls MC in his black jeans, shirt, and cut. He exuded danger, darkness, and power. What would it be like if he lost control?

Chapter 5

Saint

I sat in my office working on club business, forcing myself to not think of the woman in my playroom. I hadn't used it in a while. Kitty was the only club girl I'd played with but after she started to beg to become my old lady I'd pushed her away. Why had I put this daughter of a traitor in there? Why did I want her so badly?

Running my hand down my face, I took a deep breath, adjusted my hard cock, and once again put her out of my mind. There was endless work to get through. We had regular, some daily, shipments to our customers and distributors.

Rake was our money whiz. He could turn a dirty dollar so clean it sparkled. Their latest laundry job from the Watkins Family was a big one and would be profitable for the club.

Just as I was finishing with the stack of shipping orders, there was a sharp knock on the door. It was open but the guys knew to always provide a warning when I had my head down. No warning could cause you to end up with a bullet in your head. Looking up at who was knocking I saw one of the prospects, Crash, stuck his head around the door. in his office. "What is it?"

"Scar and Rake are back, boss."

Nodding, I stood up and followed him out to the main room just as they entered, both carrying black duffel bags. "Looks like you were successful."

"It was one of those self-storage places. This is only some of what we found. The money is all here and more. Either the additional was his or he'd been stealing from us for years," Scar growled out.

"And the product?"

"All here. He didn't do anything with it. Why steal it knowing we'd catch him? I don't get it." Rake shook his head as he pulled out bricks of coke and dope. We had a deal with the Marcos Cartel to distribute their product. This is what got Burn caught and dead. If it wasn't us then it'd have been the cartel.

Scar looked up at me. as I was staring at the haul. "You think his kid knew what he was setting aside for her?"

"No. She didn't fight for it or even want it."

"She and her friend have seen too much," Razor rasped out.

Rake growled at him over that. Raising an eyebrow I looked at Rake. Razor was dangerous even by my standards. Rake was playing with fire just by looking sideways at him.

Getting into Rake's personal space, Razor snarled at him. "Bring it, boy. I'll make you scream so loud your momma will beg for mercy."

"Get a beer, both of you. Scar, take care of this and everything else in that place. I don't want anything tying us to it. Cameras, witnesses, everything washed clean. Got me?"

"In process now. Ghost is helping."

I nodded. Ghost was our man on the inside of the FBI. He was our covert member, having been by my side as long as Scar. "Rake, join me."

He followed me into my office and closed the door behind him before sitting down. "Ella is a well-known business owner. The spotlight from her disappearance with Chastity's connection to us is too much risk of exposure for my liking. I noticed your attachment. You claiming her?"

"That's up to her."

"Provide me with a solution."

"Will do. It'll be easier if she isn't in one of those cells."

"She's your responsibility," I replied looking at him, my expression a clear warning.

"Yes, boss. Ella will ask about her friend."

I smirked at him. "She's safe for now."

Rake nodded at me as my attention returned to the stack in front of me. That was his cue to leave. While I worked on finishing up, I let my mind wander once again to Chastity Morgan. 'Soon, little blue, soon.'

***

Chastity

I sat in that room for hours. One of the guys brought me a sandwich and drink which kept me from becoming hangry. I'd even dozed off a time or two. With no windows or a way to figure out how much time had passed exactly, I was slowly going stir crazy and there had still been no sign of Saint.

A time or two I'd heard laughter, even moans of pleasure but still I waited. Was this his way of taking me out, killing me with sheer boredom? I knew I could've used the bed and just slept but the idea of sleeping in it was off-putting. I didn't want to lay in a bed where Saint had taken woman after woman, especially if one of them was the skank from earlier.

I'd finally dozed off again when the door opened and a nervous-looking man entered. He was tall like Saint but without the muscle. and raw power. Instead, he was all arms and legs, lanky and jittery. "I'm Crash, Saint wants me to move you." I narrowed my eyes on him. Something didn't sit well with me. Crash's eyes looked seemed nervous and shifty.

"Where is he moving me to? I thought he wanted me to stay here until Scar and Rake returned. Did they get what Saint wanted?" I barraged him with questions as he unlocked the cuffs and dragged me out of the room, his fingers digging into my arm. If it weren't for the colorful tattoos I had, I knew there would be fingerprint bruises left behind for every finger that dug into my arm. "I'm moving. You don't have to hold me like that, asshole."

The hard backhand to my cheek took me by surprise. None of the men had been rough with me before this, not even Saint. Sure he threatened, but not a single bruising grip or hit from any of them. Holding my cheek, my eyes filled with rage as I looked at the shithead. "Shut the fuck up, cunt," he snarled, spittle landing all over my face.

This wasn't good at all. Quickly I looked around, making note of details, trying to figure out a plan. Instead of a name on his club cut, I noticed that it said, "Prospect." With every moment that ticked by, the feeling of dread grew stronger. He opened a door leading outside and I saw a beat-up old truck waiting for us. Nora sat in the passenger seat, glaring at me.

I opened my mouth to scream when I felt something hard dig into my ribs. "Make even a peep, and I'll kill you right here. Now get into the back," Crash ordered, dragging meas he dragged over to the rear of the truck. As I was starting to climb in, I felt something hard hit the back of my head. It felt like it'd been cracked open. A moan escaped as darkness took hold.

Chapter 6

Saint

"Hey boss, did you move that girl from the black room?" I was more than ready to spend some time with Chastity and this dipshit was interrupting me, making me waste even more time.

I looked up, scowling at Slay, standing there with, a plate of food in his hand. "Why would I tell you to take her some food if I'd moved her, idiot?"

"She's not in there and I found this key on the ground next to the cuff locks." Slay handed me the key. I pulled out my keys and saw that I had the same one. There was only one key, the one I kept. There was another traitor in our midst.

My dark look grew even darker. Nora. She was known to be a vindictive bitch if she didn't get what she wanted. If she'd done something stupid, I was going to kill her. "Find me, Nora, *now*." As I watched Slay run from my office, I stood up and bellowed, "Razor, get in here!"

While I waited for him I pulled up the hidden camera footage from outside of the black room. There were hidden cameras all through the compound. Only Ranks knew about them. Sure enough, I watched as the prospect Crash dragged Chastity out of the room.

"Looks like you'll get to play tonight," I snarled, showing Razor the footage. "Check with the gate. I want to know when they left."

Razor nodded and left my office just as Slay returned. "I checked with Doc. She left saying she was fine and just wanted to rest in her room. She's not there and no one has seen her besides Doc since the fight."

"Crash has Chastity and I'd bet my left nut that the whore is with him. Find them."

I watched as Slay sat down at my computer, his fingers flying over the keys. "I'm pinging the GPS on his cell. Ever since Burn, I've made sure all club members have updated GPS on their phones."

"He left the compound in that piece of shit cage he uses. It looks like Nora was with him." Razor informed me.

"What the fuck is going on Razor? First Burn, now this. When we find them, I want them brought here alive. The club needs reminding of what betraying me and this club looks like."

"Got 'em. Maybe ten minutes out at that deserted farmhouse along the State Highway."

"Ride out. Time to go hunting."

Chastity

As I started to regain consciousness, the first thing that hit me was the pain at the back of my head. It felt like I'd been hit by a sledgehammer that was continuing to pound into my skull. A moan escaped my lips as I reached up to touch to the back of my head. I wasn't sure which dawned on me first, that my hands were tied or that there was something sticky in my hair and it was burning my eyes.

Slowly, after wiping the blood out of my eyes, I was able to focus on my surroundings. I heard two voices, one shrill and annoying. It was making the pounding in my head worse. "Drag her out here, baby. I wanna have some fun before we kill her. She needs to pay for what she did to me."

Nora. Fuck. With that knowledge, I started to remember being dragged out by some guy. I couldn't remember his name but I knew if I didn't come to my senses, I was fucked.

It didn't seem like Saint knew about this by the way they were acting. That gave me a slim bit of hope. There was some kind of covering over me. It felt like a tarp of some kind. I needed to get a look to see if I could escape this situation. I couldn't hope that a man would save me. I had to save myself.

Before I could do anything, the tarp was pulled off of me and I was thrust into the painful brightness of a Texas afternoon. My eyes watered as they tried to adjust, my head pounding. away. A painful grip on my arm hauled me from the back of the pickup truck. I was dragged a few feet away from it before being thrown onto the dirt.

In front of me were stripper heels that I recognized all too well. Looking up, I smirked, wiping more blood from my eyes. "Well, if it isn't the club whore. All you can do is lie on your back, waiting for the next cock to fill your stretched-out holes. No wonder you're such a bitch, you can't even fight for your turf properly," I taunted.

I knew I should've kept my mouth shut but I never seemed to have that ability. My mom always wanted me to get a quiet normal office job, but my mouth and that kind of work environment didn't mesh very well. I watched, smiling as my words sunk into Nora's very empty head and she screeched, attempting to slap me. I caught her hand with a snarl of my own and tackled her to the ground.

I let my rage fill me, the pain in my head fueling it, and punched Nora over and over, never letting up until she stopped moving. I slowly stood up, my head spinning, and turned around, prepared to fight Crash next. Only it was Saint that stood there with what looked like a proud smirk on his face. Crash was on his knees with Razor standing behind him.

My rage was far from sated. Ignoring that Saint and Razor were there, I attacked Crash. "Fucking son of a bitch. That pistol whip *hurt*!" Arms wrapped around my waist pulling me away from him but I wanted to claw his eyes out, I wanted to make him bleed.

I ripped myself away from Saint and turned my rage onto him. "Are you happy, you asshole? Did you recover your shit? I've been kidnapped twice, punched, pistol whipped, threatened I don't even know how many times. Forced to sit and wait in kink central to stew with my own thoughts for hours upon hours. Fuck Burn! Fuck you! I didn't want any of this!"

The small voice in the back of my head was screaming at me to shut up, but I honestly didn't care anymore. This had been a shit day from hell and I was done with all of it. My enraged eyes met Saint's smirk, and my tirade was about to begin again when out of the blue, his hands grasped my cheeks and he kissed me, hard.

At first, I tried to push him away. I didn't want to kiss him. I wanted to kick his ass. His lips drowned all that out until there was only raw passion. His tongue tangled with mine, caressing and tasting me while I clung to him. One hand released my face to wrap around my waist, pulling my body flush against his. His body was hard and oh so big. That included the rod in his pants which was was long and, thick, growing harder by the second.

Saint groaned softly as he pulled away from me. "I'm sorry about this, little blue. No one was supposed to touch you. They'll be dealt with. Let's get you back to the compound and have Doc take a look at your head."

"Am I still your prisoner? Is Ella?" I asked as he set me down onto my rather unsteady feet.

"Ella is rather occupied with Rake currently. As for you, we'll discuss that after Doc takes care of you. That head wound is deep."

I nodded as I watched as Saint removed his cut, holding it while he shrugged out of his shirt. Putting his cut back on over his shirtless chest was a crime against all of womanhood. His hard, defined pecs and abs were littered with black tattoos in a mass of images and patterns that seemed to tell the story of the man using his shirt to try to staunch the flow of blood from out of my wounded head.

"Bring them in alive," he ordered Razor who nodded with a smirk. Looking at me, he gave a slight nod. of approval. Apparently, my crazy cat-fight earned his approval. Fucked up, all of them.

Chapter 7

Saint

We arrived back at the compound and I could tell that Chastity's head wound bothered her more than she wanted to admit. Doc was there waiting and immediately sat her down, taking a look at it. "I'm going to have to stitch it up. Don't worry, sweetness, I'll numb it first, okay?"

She nodded tiredly. I held her hand as I commanded, "Razor, bring the traitors."

Razor brought Crash and Nora in.. He forced them down onto their knees in front of me. Nora was sobbing, begging for mercy but I didn't want to hear any of it. Crash just glared at me.

"This whore and her partner kidnapped a woman that was under my protection, under the protection of the club. This club is prosperous and powerful as you can tell by your wallets. I'll not be made a fool of or let this club be betrayed. Chastity is mine and anyone who attacks what is mine attacks me."

"Aye!" came the rousing reply from the club members.

Turning to look at Nora, I pulled out my pistol and put a bullet between her eyes. "Razor, take Crash to the basement. He is yours. Dispose of the trash and every club girl will clean the stain upon this club. I expect it to be gone."

Turning back to Chastity, I was unsure what I would see in her eyes. Would she be upset by what I did? Would she be repulsed? No, what I saw was a glint of hardness, with a nod she told me, "It is done."

Chastity

I woke up the next morning, being held close by Saint. He was a cuddler, which surprised the fuck out of me. He hadn't tried anything all night. I'd fallen asleep almost instantly from sheer exhaustion. I rolled over and looked at the man holding me. Asleep, he had an almost a boyish quality to his face. Reaching up, my finger softly caressed the curves of his face.

"Creeping on me while I sleep, little blue?" The sound of his raspy, sleep-filled voice made me shiver. It screamed sex appeal.

"Maybe," I smiled. For several moments we got lost in each other's eyes. "By right, I should hate you," I whispered.

"You should. I'm not a good man, Chastity. There's a darkness in me filled with cruelty, but around you, I feel a sense of peace and rightness that I've never felt before. I'm too old to change the path my life has taken but I find myself wanting what I don't deserve."

"And what is that?"

"You. I want you."

"I'm not a weak female that trembles and cries because of the scary big bad wolf. If anything, I'm the girl who thinks the wolf was way hotter than the hunter any ole day. I can't do this if one day I turn around to find you've left like Burn left me as a child. I just can't. It would break me beyond repair." I closed my eyes, fighting back the emotion I didn't want to feel then.

Saint leaned close, softly capturing my lips before he said against them, "I don't want that either, baby. If we do this, I want forever."

"Forever is good, but if I'm going to have forever with a Saint, I should at least know his name before I worship at his altar." My hand caressed his length under the blanket, knowing what I wanted.

"Luciano Telos."

"Saint Lucifer," I murmured against his lips. Rolling me onto my back, Saint's lips placed kisses and nips along my jaw and down my neck all the way to my collarbone. Everywhere he touched created little explosions of pleasure.

"You taste like heaven," he said against my neck. "Are you going to let the Devil corrupt you, my angel?"

"Yes," I moaned as he captured my lips in a kiss that would make Mother Teresa beg for mercy. Moving my hands to the edge of his shirt, I broke the kiss to pull it off. remove it before kissing him again.

My fingers grazed over his chiseled torso and I knew I'd let this man corrupt me all day, every day. My body started to heat up as Saint's fingers grazed my skin while he removed my shirt. Underneath I wore a light blue lace bra. over an ample bosom and a petite body.

Saint growled when he discovered at seeing that I wore matching lace boy shorts. "Beautiful. A body built to tempt the devil. You're my fallen angel and only mine." His arms wrapped around me, pulling me to him, as he kissed me.

"My Saint is a naughty boy."

"Always," he replied huskily, sucking and nipping at the tender skin on my neck.

I rolled him over onto his back, pushing him down as I slid my body down his, until I reached his jeans. I unzipped them,began opening his jeans, licking and tasting his exposed skin. His jeans gave way and I pushed them down towards the end of the bed, exposing his fully erect cock.

Taking it in my hands, I massaged and toyed with him, causing him to groan. I took him deep into my mouth and throat, his moan making me drip. "Fuck." He groaned as I licked and suckled, tugged, and pulled. I brought him to the very edge before releasing him with a pop.

I stood up, as Saint watched me through hooded eyes as I took a half-step away from him and then slowly removed my bra and lace shorts, hoping it was as sexy and seductive as I wanted it to be. His eyes caressed my skin, making me feel sexy. "Condom?" I asked.

"Nightstand," he growled, his dark eyes never leaving my body. Grabbing one from the top draw I climbed over his body and settled over his thighs. "Baby, you are so fucking hot. Slide that condom over my cock and climb aboard. Because I'm going to take you over and over today, and by the time dinner rolls around there will be no doubt that you are mine and only mine."

I smiled at him, my dripping wet pussy making his thighs wet. Rolling the condom over his cock the small voice in my head wondered if he was even going to fit. Climbing over him, I positioned him at my opening and slowly slid him into my body. The stretch and burn morphed into pleasure and as my eyes rolled back into my head. "Yes," I purred. at him.

With a possessive growl, that one simple word removed what remained of his control. He suddenly flipped us over and held me in his arms, kissing me hungrily as he pushed me back down onto the bed. "Mine.," he moaned in her ear.

"Claim me, make me yours and only yours, my Lucifer," I begged, wrapping my legs around his waist..

In response to my request, he pulled almost all the way out before he thrust back into my body, causing me to moan when he went further than anyone had before. Every thrust, In and out he moved, each time harder and deeper, his hands massaging my breasts and teasing my nipples while he kissed me. He hit the end of me, causing me to moan louder at the mix of pleasure and pain that filled me as his dick kissed my cervix. "Don't hold back, never hold back with me.," I moaned.

He rolled us over again so that I was on top once more. I grabbed hold of the headboard, riding him hard and fast. His hands grabbed hold of my breasts. He alternated his mouth between each nipple, licking and tasting me, placing love bites on my tender skin, my eyes closed in pleasure.

Reaching down between us with one hand, with one hand down between us, he found my clit and rubbed it, causing pleasure to explode with a scream. My body convulsed and squeezed around him as he gritted his teeth to keep from joining me, the look on his face told me that he wasn't done with me yet.

Saint

Pulling out of her luscious body, I couldn't help smiling at her groan of complaint. Once was never going to be enough with this woman. I couldn't wait to take her to my playroom. I was going to make her beg for mercy. Flipping her over, I pulled her up onto her hands and knees before plunging back into her, my arms wrapping around her waist as I reached down and once again pleasured her.

"My woman, my feisty Chastity," I whispered into her ear, as each thrust becoming harder. The faster I moved, the louder she moaned, each thrust setting off micro-orgasms in her body.

"My Saint, my Lucifer," she cried loudly as she came in wave after wave.

My movements became erratic and my balls were heavy. I knew I was close. Finally, with one hard thrust, I couldn't hold back anymore. Pushing into her as deep as possible, I filled the condom, knowing that one day soon I was going to take her bare, my seed painting the walls of her pussy.

We finally collapsed onto the bed, panting. Holding her in my arms I smiled. Seeing my smile, Chastity caressed my lips with shaky fingers. "I'll be your fallen angel forever."

Nipping at her neck, I groaned into her ear, "You smell like vanilla and taste like heaven." I held her close to me as we rested, both of us drifting off to sleep.

Chastity

Saint led me down the hall to his black room. He had me wear a shirt of his while he wore a loose pair of jeans. We entered the room and he locked the door so that we wouldn't be disturbed. We'd been hiding from everyone, wanting to spend the day alone.

"When we're in this room there are rules, little blue," he stated with dominance as he spun me around.

He retrieved a long piece of red silk and placed it over my eyes, tying it in place at the back of my head. I could feel his fingers skimming down my body until they reached the hem of the shirt I wore. He pulled it up and over my head, making sure the silk was still firmly in place.

I was naked, vulnerable, and blindfolded. "Saint, I…" I whispered.

"Silence, Chastity. I'll explain what I'm going to do and in this room, you'll always be safe." His dark commanding voice made me shudder with anticipation. "In our bedroom, I am Saint or Luciano. Here I am Master and I'll bring you more pleasure than you've ever encountered before. Tell me you understand," he rasped in my ear.

I was shivering with desire, willing to do anything he wanted, even if he was pushing me out of my comfort zone. "Yes, Master," I answered. My voice sounded thick with lust.

"Now for a safe word. One that you'll use whenever you wish to stop what we're doing."

"Yellow." I don't know why I chose that word but I knew it wasn't one I'd ever scream in pleasure.

"Yellow it is."

Something soft brushed my skin and I let out a soft, surprised gasp. It was silky and cool, like the petals of a rosebud trailing from the top of my forehead, tracing my nose, lips, and chin, caressing the dip in my neck before continuing its journey down my body. My breath stuttered as a plethora of sensations overwhelmed me. Suddenly, Saint's mouth was on me, causing me to gasp in surprise, and then he was gone.

I heard the sounds of chains and nervously turned my head in the direction it came from. He took each of my wrists in hand and attached the cuffs as he had before. This time though, when he was finished, my arms were pulled up over my head until I was raised up onto my toes.

"This time, little blue, we'll take it slow and steady. We'll explore more sensations each time we come to this room. Today though, you will learn that trusting your master brings nothing but pleasure." He lifted me, guiding my legs to wrap around his waist. I felt like I was floating freely in the air. That is until he thrust his cock into me hard and fast as he pinched my bud. I screamed in pleasure and knew that I would want to come into this room, again and again.

Epilogue

Chastity

I couldn't help but smirk at the tattoo I was doing. This was going to be my all-time favorite. "How does it look, little blue?"

"I like it. Any female that sees this baby is going to know who you belong to." I leaned down close to his ear, warning laced in my voice, "But no woman will ever see it. Am I clear, Lucifer?"

Saint turned his head to look at me, his eyes dark. "Seems to me someone needs a visit from her Master so she knows that she's the only one for me."

"Yes, please," I begged, kissing him hard. Pulling away, I smacked the cheek I wasn't tattooing, "Turn over so I can finish my property tag." Saint chuckled at me as he resettled, his eyes closing as the sting of the tattoo gun relaxed him.

A short while later, I was cleaning up when his phone rang. "Yeah?" he answered. I watched as his eyebrows furrowed, a dangerous look on his face. "Fucking Hell! How many?"

"Bring them to the basement. Hell's MC wants war, they'll get war!"

I watched nervously as he hung up. "What's happened?" Saint never told me the specifics of their club business but I knew the basics. I knew the guys had a big delivery of guns to the Marcos Cartel.

"Hell's Last Stand attacked the delivery. Shot our guys up before they knew what hit them. Scar has been hit and it's bad. They're bringing them to the compound. We need to go."

I nodded, locking as I quickly locked up the shop. "Razor?" The enforcer and I had developed a sort of rapport and I didn't want to see both him and Scar hurt.

"Razor was grazed but nothing bad. He was able to capture one of their guys, Vic, and his daughter. We'll get the answers we need."

I nodded. I hated this part of the club life but I would stand by Saint's side as his Old Lady and support him in any way I could. "Let's go, the club needs us. Hell's MC will pay, you'll make sure of it." I kissed him hard on the lips.

"My fallen angel, let's go show those motherfuckers what it means to mess with the Dragon Skulls MC!"

THE END

About the Authors

Euryia Larsen grew up thinking that what she was being told about the world was only part of the story. She loves myths both historical and modern and often sees the the possibility in 'what if'. A good romance with strong 'alpha' heroes and even stronger heroines that can be a partner for them are her favorite kinds of books. If the heroines are just a tad crazy, even better.

Euryia is a stay at home mom of two beautiful daughters, three crazy cats, three crazier dogs and a husband to round out the bunch. She deals with her fair share of issues while dealing with Fibromyalgia and other complications and as a result, she's finds an escape in books where there is always a happily ever after. She's always been creative and has written for herself as an audience for longer than she can remember.

I'd love to hear your thoughts on this or myths or books in general or even just a hello.

Check me out at
http://www.EuryiaLarsen.com

Kyra Nyx proves that Happily Ever Afters aren't reserved for knights in shining armor. Her heroes swagger in, drag you into the gray area, and make you rethink your fairy tale. Follow these interconnected stories and get swept away by heroes who put romance on the edge.

Kyra Nyx - Facebook:
https://www.facebook.com/AuthorKyraNyx/

Other Books by Euryia Larsen

Broken Butterfly Dreams

Standalone Novellas:

The Mobster's Violet

Clover's Luck

Touch of Gluttony

Halloween Darkness

Another Notch On Her Toolbelt

Sealed With A Kiss

Fate's Surprise

Midnight Rose

His Curvy Housemaid

Hello, Goodbye

The Dark Side (Dragon Skulls MC):

Saint

Beautiful Smile

Twisted Savior

Belladonna Club:

To Trap A Kiss

His Peridot

Zima Family:

Devil's Desire

Cursed Angel

Baranov Bratva:

Sinful Duty

Sweet Child of Mine

Menage Series:

Masked Surprise

Sweet Cherry Pie

Home on the Ranch

Perfect Storm

Curveball

Lonesome Shadows

Cursed Guardians

Love is Love Boxsets:

Menage A Trois

Affaire de Coeur

Not the Good Guy (Kazon Brothers)

with Kyra Nyx:

<u>Kazon Brothers Box Set</u>

<u>The Dark</u>

<u>The Beast</u>

<u>The Villain</u>

Saga of The Realms:

<u>Power of Love – Prequel Novella (Paperback)</u>

<u>Power of Love – Prequel Novella (Free Ebook)</u>

<u>Bonded By Destiny</u>

<u>War of Giants</u>

Printed in Great Britain
by Amazon